To Ruth x

First published 2009 by Macmillan Children's Books
a division of Macmillan Publishers Limited
20 New Wharf Road, London N1 9RR
Basingstoke and Oxford
Associated companies throughout the world
www.panmacmillan.com

ISBN: 978-0-230-70147-2 (hb)
ISBN: 978-0-230-70186-1 (pb)

Text and illustrations copyright © Natalie Russell 2009
Moral rights asserted

1 3 5 7 9 8 6 4 2

A CIP catalogue record for this book is available from the British Library.

Printed in Malaysia

natalie russell

moon rabbit

THE PARK

THE CITY

MACMILLAN CHILDREN'S BOOKS

Little Rabbit liked living in the city.

She had her own place to stay,
her favourite cafe and so many
things to see and do.

But at night, when everything was quiet and
Little Rabbit was all alone, she would look up at
the moon and wonder if there was someone out there.

THEATRE

Someone she could play with,
laugh with and have fun with.

Someone just like her.

It would be nice to meet another
little rabbit, she thought.

When the city became very busy,
Little Rabbit would go to the
park to read her book.

One day, as Little Rabbit read, she heard the most beautiful music floating on the air. She lay back and listened.

The park was so peaceful and the sun was so warm that Little Rabbit's eyes began to close and very soon she was fast asleep.

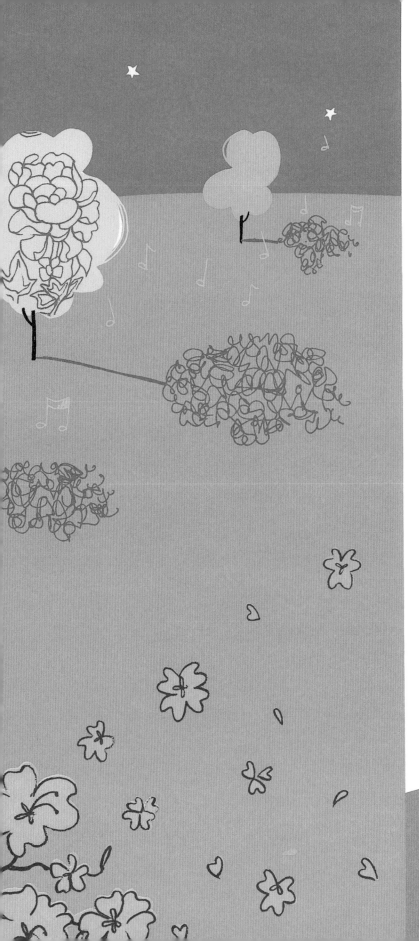

When Little Rabbit woke up, the sun had gone and the moon was shining brightly. It was past Little Rabbit's bedtime.

But in the distance she could still hear music and it was the kind of music she liked.

So Little Rabbit picked up her book and followed the sound through the trees. And there she saw . . .

a rabbit!

A brown rabbit who was playing a guitar, making music that made Little Rabbit want to dance.

So she stayed for a while.

As Brown Rabbit played,
Little Rabbit danced.

Then Little Rabbit told tales of the city and Brown Rabbit listened.

Together they watched the changing moon until the birds sang to the morning sun.

And for a while Little Rabbit forgot about her life back in the city.

The two rabbits had picnics
in the sunshine

and games of
hide-and-seek.

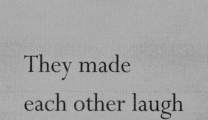

They made
each other laugh

and Little Rabbit was happy
to have found a new friend.

But then, one dark night, Little Rabbit saw the city
lights glowing in the distance and suddenly felt sad.

"The city is so beautiful," she sighed.

Brown Rabbit was quiet. How could anything be
as beautiful as the moonlit park, he thought.

Brown Rabbit didn't like to
see his new friend feeling sad,
so he played his guitar

and danced around Little Rabbit.

But there was nothing he could do to make her happy.

"It's time for me to go home," said Little Rabbit.

He even stood on his head. Anything to make her laugh or to see her smile.

So, early the next morning,
Little Rabbit returned to the city.

Back to her home, back to her favourite cafe and
back to all the things she liked to see and do.

And she no longer gazed at the moon and wondered if there was someone out there.

Another little rabbit just like her.

Because she knew that there was.

And he was coming to visit the very next day.

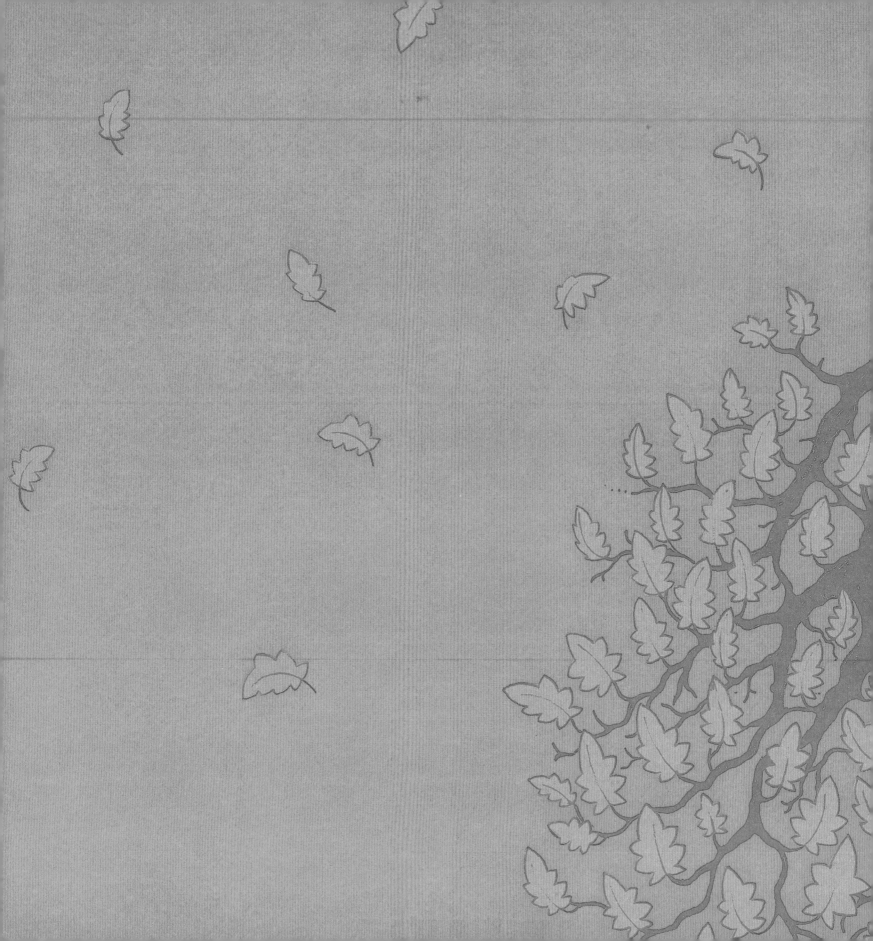